Barn on Fire

Heather Amery

Illustrated by Stephen Cartwright

Language consultant: Betty Root
Series editor: Jenny Tyler

There is a little yellow duck to find on every page.

This is Apple Tree Farm.

This is Mrs. Boot, the farmer. She has two children, called Poppy and Sam, and a dog called Rusty.

This is Ted.

Ted works at Apple Tree Farm. He looks after
the tractor and all the other farm machines.

Poppy and Sam help Ted.

They like helping Ted with jobs on the farm. Today
he is fixing the fence around the sheep field.

Sam smells smoke.

"Ted," says Sam, "I think something's burning."
Ted stops working and they all sniff hard.

The barn is on fire.

"Look," says Poppy, "there's smoke coming from the hay barn. It must be on fire. What shall we do?"

"Call a fire engine."

"Come on," says Ted. "Run to the house. We must call a fire engine. Run as fast as you can."

Poppy and Sam run to the house.

"Help!" shouts Poppy. "Call a fire engine.
Quickly! The hay barn is on fire."

Mrs. Boot dials the number.

"It's Apple Tree Farm," she says. "A fire engine please, as fast as you can. Thank you very much."

"You must stay here."

"Now, Poppy," says Mrs. Boot. "I want you and
Sam to stay indoors. And don't let Rusty out."

Poppy and Sam watch from the door.

Soon they hear the siren. Then the fire engine roars up the road and into the farmyard.

"The firemen are here."

The firemen jump down from the engine.
They lift down lots of hoses and unroll them.

The firemen run over to the barn with the hoses.
Can you see where they get the water from?

The firemen squirt water onto the barn.

Poppy and Sam watch them from the window.
"It's still burning on the other side," says Poppy.

"There's the fire."

One fireman runs behind the barn. What a surprise!
Two campers are cooking on a big wood fire.

The fire is out.

"We're sorry," say the campers. "It was exciting," says Sam, "but I'm glad the barn is all right."

Cover design by Hannah Ahmed   Digital manipulation by Natacha Goransky

This edition first published in 2004 by Usborne Publishing Ltd, 83-85 Saffron Hill, London EC1N 8RT, England. www.usborne.com